dot

Peter H. Reynolds

WALKER BOOKS
AND SUBSIDIARIES
LONDON · BOSTON · SYDNEY · AUCKLAND

The art class was over, but Vashti sat glued to her chair.

Her paper was empty.

Vashti's teacher leaned
over the blank paper.

"Ah! A polar bear
in a snow storm," she said.

"Very funny!" said Vashti.
"I just CAN'T draw!"

Her teacher smiled.

"Just make a mark and
see where it takes you."

Vashti grabbed a felt-tipped pen and gave the paper a good, strong jab.

"There!"

Her teacher picked up the paper
and studied it carefully.

"Hmmmmm."

She pushed the paper towards
Vashti and quietly said,
"Now sign it."

Vashti thought for a moment.

"Well, maybe I can't draw,
but I CAN sign my name."

The next week,
when Vashti walked into her art class,
she was surprised to see what was
hanging above her teacher's desk.

It was the little dot
she had drawn—HER DOT!
All framed in swirly gold!

"Hmmph!
I can make a better dot
than THAT!"

She opened her
never-before-used set of
watercolours and set to work.

Vashti painted and painted.
A red dot.
A purple dot.
A yellow dot.
A blue dot.

The blue mixed with the yellow.
She discovered that she could make
a GREEN dot.

Vashti kept experimenting.
Lots of little dots in many colours.

"If I can make little dots,
I can make BIG dots, too."

Vashti splashed her colours with
a bigger brush on bigger paper
to make bigger dots.

Vashti even made a dot
by NOT painting a dot.

At the school art show a few weeks later,
Vashti's many dots made quite a splash.

Vashti noticed a little boy
gazing up at her.

"You're a really great artist.
I wish I could draw," he said.

"I bet you can," said Vashti.

"ME? No, not me. I can't draw
a straight line with a ruler."

Vashti smiled.

She handed the boy a
blank sheet of paper.
"Show me."

The boy's pencil shook
as he drew his line.

Vashti stared at the boy's squiggle.
And then she said . . .

"sign it."

Dedicated to Mr. Matson, my 7th grade math teacher,
who dared me to "make my mark."

First published 2003 by Walker Books Ltd
87 Vauxhall Walk, London SE11 5HJ

This edition published 2004

29 28 27 26 25 24 23 22

© 2003, 2004 Peter H. Reynolds

This book has been handlettered by Peter H. Reynolds

Printed in China

British Library Cataloguing in Publication Data: a catalogue record for
this book is available from the British Library.

ISBN 978-1-84428-169-5

www.walker.co.uk